D1373284

"As an educator of 28 years, I have seen a dramatic increase in the need for increased attention to mindfulness and self-care. Dr. Bhatt has been a leader in my community as an advocate for wellness and a friend to so many. I have been fortunate enough to tap into his expertise for my own health and the health of my family. Knowing the stress educators have been under, Dr. Bhatt has generously done volunteer work for my faculty. The story of Kenzi will be a fun way for young minds to grow and develop a sense of empowerment while recognizing the importance of making a positive difference in their communities. I have seen the impact of stress on our students. It is imperative that we provide them with the tools to thrive and manage stress as a normal part of life. I know Dr. Bhatt's words and wisdom will be a fantastic place for anyone to start."

— JOHN SLOAN

PRINCIPAL, CEDAR PARK HIGH SCHOOL

"As a mother and a physician who treats spine-related issues, I full-heartedly endorse this book and the message and education in it. Dr. Bhatt (aka Bhattman) is on the cutting edge of health care when it comes to pain and wellness. His approach is positive, holistic, and very accessible. Dr. Bhatt's book is filled with excitement and energy that children will instantly respond to positively. This book is a must-read for not just children but also their parents who have seen their own health and posture decline as a result of this pandemic."

— AI MUKAI, MD

BOARD CERTIFIED IN PHYSICAL MEDICINE AND
REHABILITATION AND PAIN MEDICINE, TEXAS ORTHOPEDICS
AND SPORTS REHABILITATION; AFFILIATE FACULTY,
UNIVERSITY OF TEXAS, AUSTIN, DELL MEDICAL SCHOOL

"As the Chief Revenue Officer of a large health-care IT company, I realized it is more important now to take care of our minds and our bodies. With more people working from home and with the current state of Covid, we are spending a lot of our day sitting at desks in an unnatural position. I know this has created pain in my back, neck, and shoulders. Dr. Mike Bhatt has been a friend for over 20 years and has always been a huge help to me personally. I asked Mike to do a series with my company, HealthEdge, so that he could help countless others through his 7-minute huddle. It was a great way for my colleagues to get up, stretch, meditate, and keep moving during their busy day. There has been so much positive feedback that dozens have asked me when Dr. Bhatt is coming back! This is a program for any age, and I can remember a teacher from my past that used to get us up twice during the day to stretch and move. I never forgot that lesson and I know today's youth can benefit from Dr. Bhatt's teachings. I can't wait to share *Kenzi Sits Up Tall* with everyone I know! It's a brilliant book and so simple to establish into your daily routine."

—CHRIS CONTE
CHIEF REVENUE OFFICER AND EXECUTIVE
VICE PRESIDENT, HEALTHEDGE

"*Kenzi Sits Up Tall* is exceptional!! Not only is it a fun read, but it is also so informative. Being a mother of three kids, I want to teach them healthy habits, and I learned so much too! We should all sit up tall!"

—KRISTINA LACKEY SRE,
PTA, STEINER RANCH ELEMENTARY

KENZI
SITS UP TALL

written by
Mike Bhatt

Illustrated by
Iman Jordan

RIVER GROVE
BOOKS

Published by River Grove Books
Austin, TX
www.rivergrovebooks.com

Distributed by River Grove Books

Design and composition by Greenleaf Book Group and Iman Jordan
Cover design by Greenleaf Book Group and Iman Jordan

Publisher's Cataloging-in-Publication data is available.

Print ISBN: 978-1-63299-635-0

eBook ISBN: 978-1-63299-636-7

First Edition

There are so many people to dedicate this book to. I would firstly like to thank my parents. They are my inspiration for being hardworking, dedicated immigrants who took the leap of faith many years ago by leaving their homeland for greener pastures. Seeing the struggles and challenges that they battled and conquered are always an inspiration for me and has made me a stronger and more dedicated person and doctor. I also thank my clinical mentors Dr. Bill Defoyd and Dr. Buddy Tipton for always making me think outside of the box. I also dedicate this book to Kirk Leavell. Kirk, you taught me so much about exercise and fitness, and you are so missed, my friend. Rest in strength. Thanks to the Lackey family for allowing me to always see the best in people and to keep pushing the needle a little more.

AUTHOR'S NOTE

The theme for my illustrated kids' book is to teach good posture, breathing, and mental health to children and adolescents via the mind, body, and spirit in a simple seven-minute-a-day program called the 7-minute huddle. I have been a practicing chiropractor for thirty years and have seen all variations and trends in musculoskeletal injuries associated with occupational hazards, which have more recently been affecting our younger population.

As a result of the pandemic and even prior, I began noticing in my private practice a significant spike in the number of children and adolescents suffering from back pain, neck pain, headaches, and anxiety. I wanted a simple way to spread the message that there are easy ways to help prevent having to visit a medical physician, physical therapist, or chiropractor, and to place self-care in the hands of every parent and child. The main character in this book is a girl named Kenzi. She has many talents that are placed in jeopardy due to various conditions similar to what I have seen recently in our youth.

I am known to my patients and many others as Dr. Bhattman. Dr. Bhattman educates, entertains, and advises children with helpful advice and strategies to stay healthy and strong.

Mommy's own neck and back had, in the past, caused her pain.
But when her doctor helped her, a pain-free life she did gain.
That night at bedtime she whispered, as she gave me a hug.
"I'LL TAKE YOU TO DR. BHATTMAN, my little love bug."

We went to his clinic and, **WOW** I felt better!
The answer so simple, I could now be a **TRENDSETTER.**
Dr. Bhattman taught me a plan called the

7-MINUTE HUDDLE.

It all made so much sense, I gave my parents a cuddle.

The program was educational and **FUN.**
I found it **SO EASY** to get it all done.
Daddy then asked what I thought about my visit.
With a smile on my face, I answered,

"EXQUISITE!"

THREE SIMPLE LESSONS

did Dr. Bhattman relay.
He smiled wide, and to me,
this **little message**
he did say:

"care for **MIND** & **BODY**, and keep your **SPIRIT** light."

In only **seven minutes,** you'll **start your day right.**

"TWO MINUTES to be mindful, and **breathing is the start.**

FOUR MINUTES for the body, **stretching the spine** a major part."

"And the last one is my **FAVORITE**," he admitted with a grin. "ONE MINUTE to UPLIFT SOMEONE and make their SPIRIT GLAD." I mean, duh, **WHAT A GREAT** SEVEN MINUTES WE HAD!

The first thing he taught on my back I was to lie.
I stretch out my arms with my PALMS TO THE SKY.
Next, I close my eyes and think a joyous thought.

SMILE BIG

to deal with whatever the school day brought.

BREATHE DEEEEEP

from my belly, my lungs getting bigger.
More air coming in—I can handle any trigger.
Breathe in through my nose and out of my mouth—

SUCCESS!

Oxygen to my brain and body,
and gone is my stress!

A model of the spine he brought for me to see,
but its **SLOUCHING** was so bad!

Bones, joints, and muscles all
CROOKED, I could tell
—its appearance was quite sad.

"SIT TALL IN YOUR CHAIR,"
the doctor said next.

"STRETCH TO THE SKY,
with your arms nice and high.
Tuck your chin backward and open your chest."

Doing these exercises makes me

FEEL MY BEST!

And last but not least is to be

THOUGHTFUL & KIND.

Only a minute required
to center my mind.

"DANDY DEEDS,"

Dr. Bhattman calls them,
and I think they're a gem.

I get to think of ways to

BE KIND to another.

Friendships in store waiting to discover.

Care for **MIND** and **BODY**, and
keep your **SPIRIT** light.
In only **7 MINUTES**,
you'll start your day right.

With this wisdom from Dr. Bhattman, my eyes opened wide.
My friends had the same **problems,** and I could stand by their side.
That day I knew it . . . and this I recall,

that helping my friends was IMP**O**RTANT for all.
Frustration was mounting in everyone's lives.
I wanted all to know we could **do better than just survive.**

I gathered a group of my friends on the double,
then announced nice and loud,

"I'M HERE TO STOP THE TROUBLE!"

with my **BODY** and **MIND** now nice and loose,
I offered suggestions to put to **good use**.

Dr. Bhattman's **7-MINUTE HUDDLE**—
what I've learned is truly key . . .
to be kind to myself and others—
I'm sure you would

AGREE.

My friend Suzie and I, we both play the flute.
But when we **sat slouched,**
you could barely hear a TOOT.
The day of the recital was quickly drawing near.

A problem to solve.
OH MY!
OH, DEAR!

I told my friend Suzie,
"Let's sit up tall, because no doubt
when we fill our lungs fuller,
a **LOUDER SOUND** will come out."
Then we blew into our flutes and our music was heard.
We each sounded like a beautiful

SONGBIRD!

The people in the crowd all smiled
when we were done.
Our friends and teachers were so proud
of the **awards we'd won!**

My friends and I thought we'd try something new.
Our teachers were on board and told us,

"WOOHOO!"

Since we all love to sing, dance, and act,
we would try and that indeed is a fact. . .
So we set our sights HIGH and we planned
to audition for a play, that was our pact.

But then our NERVES kicked in, oh yes, they did.
My friends would doubt, saying,

"I'M ONLY A KID."

I explained, as I'd heard from my good doctor friend,
that our talents were within us, this was not a **DEAD END.**
As Dr. Bhattman explained, when our fears do advance,
step up to the plate and tell them,

"GOOD RIDDANCE!"

TO BREATHE DEEP

from our bellies, focus, and visualize.
This will launch **HAPPY FEELINGS** to help win the prize.

My friends and I, we aced the audition.
This simple plan helped us to
CONQUER OUR MISSION.

We finished on stage with big smiles and stood tall. Our minds were so fresh—
ENOUGH HAPPINESS FOR ALL.

We like to play soccer, and **DINOS** is our team.
Sometimes after games, we get to go out for ice cream.
With the season approaching
I was EXCITED to dive in,
kick that ball hard,
and help my team

WIN!

But when my muscles felt tight,
I couldn't run as fast.
Soccer no longer
felt like such a

BLAST.

After STRETCHING my hamstrings,
I regained my speed.
Slow running was now in the past, indeed.

Out onto the field with a

WHOOP

and a scream,
I kicked the ball to my friend
and we played as a team.

My crew and I, we have this dear FRIEND,
and he had a problem we helped him to mend.
His name is Akash, and we were all great buds,
but his choice to be inactive was truly a dud.

Akash was on his computer for HOURS on end.
Missing fresh air and movement was sadly his trend.
We would ask him to come out, but his answer was no.
To PLAY outdoors, he would not go.

But one day we all got **TOGETHER** to see
if we asked him as a group, could we set him free?
Standing tall by his window, we asked him at last,
"Come on, Akash! Let's go have a blast!"

Akash turned off his computer
and came out that day with us.
His smiling face was surely a plus.
He said, "Okay, let's go to the park!"
Playing outside lit within him a

SPARK.

The lessons of the 7-minute Huddle are so good.

FEELING GREAT,

I want to follow them as often as I should.
Every day, remembering to take
deep belly breaths is easy.
And I can do it in class—
it's not even cheesy.

I remind myself to SIT TALL and tuck in my chin.
Then show love to my classmates and, together,

WE ALL WIN!

I can tackle the day and handle any need.
When we apply the 7-minute Huddle, we are sure to

SUCCEED!

Care for mind and body, and keep your spirit light.
IN ONLY SEVEN MINUTES,
you'll start your day right!

FUN FACTS

1. The biggest bone in the body is the **FEMUR**.

2. There are **206** bones in the body.

3. The strongest muscles in the body are the **GLUTEAL** muscles.

4. It takes more muscles to **FROWN** than it does to **SMILE**.

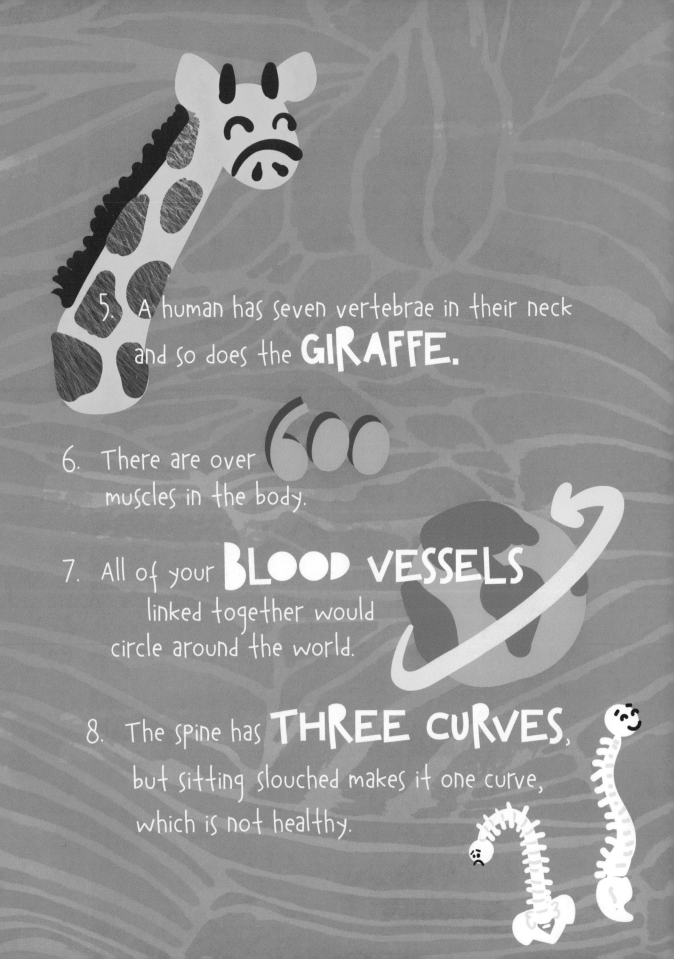

5. A human has seven vertebrae in their neck and so does the **GIRAFFE.**

6. There are over 600 muscles in the body.

7. All of your **BLOOD VESSELS** linked together would circle around the world.

8. The spine has **THREE CURVES,** but sitting slouched makes it one curve, which is not healthy.

THE 7-MINUTE HUDDLE

My name is Kenzi. Dr. Bhattman taught me three simple things to do in only 7 minutes. These things helped me be a better kid during the recent pandemic and forever after. It is so easy to make your brain, body, and spirit better with this simple plan! I hope that you enjoy doing it as much as I do.

-LOVE, KENZI

The 7-minute huddle I refer to in this book is a great tool to use with your kids and even for yourself. The structure of the seven minutes is as follows:

For the first two minutes, sit up tall and practice deep breathing. While breathing in and out, keep your mind focused on your breath and on what you see, feel, and hear around you in the present moment. Think only about the now. Work with your child to build up to two minutes of mindfulness, proper breathing technique, and visualization. Try beginning with smaller increments if necessary at first.

For the next four minutes, practice different body stretches and strengthening exercises. Stretch the legs, arms, back, and neck, holding each stretch for thirty seconds without bouncing. Next, we progress to specific exercises that strengthen our posture-specific muscle groups. Feel like your posture makes you taller from the top of your head to the sky. Refer to the QR code below to access videos that provide stage one of postural correction exercises: stretch, strengthen, and stabilize.

Finally, for the last minute, brainstorm with your child how they might be able to uplift someone in their life. Consider relatives, neighbors, peers, and even strangers (with parental monitoring, of course). Simple acts of kindness can go a long way to changing the mood or outlook of the recipient. Remember to teach our kids that we sometimes never know what might be going on in someone's life and how our actions can change someone's day for the better!

Consistency is important in the 7-minute huddle, so ideally, find a similar time each day that you can do a 7-Minute Huddle with your child until they are ready to practice on their own.

Thank you for your purchase! Please use this QR code to view and enjoy videos on basic breathing techniques, posture exercises, Dandy Deeds, and much more!!

—LOVE, KENZI

ACKNOWLEDGMENTS

I would like to thank the following people in the creation of this book. Most importantly are all my patients over the years who have trusted in my care and have been an integral part of helping make me a better doctor, person, and advocate for their needs. I want to thank my parents for always showing me how to be a good person and have a kind heart, to always respect and honor integrity and the power of karma. I also want to thank Marta, Rusty, Alicia, and many others for letting me hound them with questions, thoughts, and critical thinking feedback. I am so eternally grateful to not only these people but so many more who I want to tell: You make life amazing by always supporting my efforts, visions, and creations. I hope that kids and youth and adults find benefit from incorporating information from the simple but so very important and effective lessons taught in this illustrated children's book.